Rocky Road Rhymes

By

Julie Sheldon

Contents

****

Introduction

Welcome to my second book of rhymes written during the Covid19 pandemic.

At the time of publishing (February 2021), I can't believe that this time last year, we had only just begun to hear vague mutterings of some mysterious virus in China.....it all seemed so very far away, and no one could have imagined that a year later the whole world would have been battling with that same virus for so long! Unfortunately, I think we still have a long way to go before we can get on with anything resembling 'normal' life.

I also can't quite believe that I have, during this time, written enough poems to publish, not one, but now, two books! This time last year, it wasn't something that I had ever considered doing, but as the last twelve months have proved...... you never know what's going to happen in life.

As in my first book, 'Lockdown Lyrics', I have continued to gain inspiration from the pandemic situation, my local surroundings, and personal thoughts and experiences. In this book, I have generally presented the poems in the order in which they were written, (between September 2020 and January 2021), as I think this shows how my thoughts and moods changed and evolved throughout the months.

I would once again like to thank my friends and family, and the people who have followed my poetry on the local village, and other poetry Facebook pages, for their ongoing encouragement and support.

As a result of publishing my first book, I have made contact with some lovely people, and reconnected with some old friends, both in person and through social media. I would like to say thank you to a fellow poet, Mark Shifflet, from Maryland, USA, who I 'met' through a Facebook poetry group....we co-wrote a couple of the poems included in this book.

I hope better days lie ahead for us all, and you never know, at this rate, I may even have enough material for another collection in the future!

I really hope you enjoy the book!

****

When deciding on a title for this book, I wanted to reflect the situation at the time of publishing, in February 2021, and felt that, the past year had been, and continued to be, a journey travelled on a rocky road…..

Rocky Road

We're travelling on a rocky road
With Covid in our midst
We're striving to escape from it
With every turn and twist

We're travelling on a rocky road
With Covid at our heels
Sometimes we're crawling on our knees
But then we find our wheels

We're travelling on a rocky road
With Covid in our sight
We must not let it rule our lives
We must put up a fight

We're travelling on a rocky road
With Covid in the throng
We're trying to keep our distance....
Avoid it and stay strong

We're travelling on a rocky road
With Covid on the loose
Sometimes it seems impassable
It's one we did not choose

We're travelling on a rocky road
With Covid by our side
We've got to try to overtake....
Don't let it hitch a ride

We're travelling on a rocky road
With Covid on our tail
We must not let it catch us up
We have to make it fail

We're travelling on a rocky road
With Covid on the chase
We need to make a final push
And try to win the race!

****

One of the things I seem to notice on TV these days is that so many people seem to have smiles that are too perfect and too white. My Dad has always had a gap between his front teeth and it is just one of the lovely quirky things that I think makes him 'him'. He'd look ridiculous with 'perfect' teeth!.....

Perfect Teeth

I know it's good to have nice teeth......But things have gone too far!
The dazzling, perfect gnashers of......The film and TV stars....

Remind me of the 'sixties' when......I was but just a child....
And everyone past forty five......Had matching pearly smiles!

They had all teeth extracted then......Before, out, they did fall
Their dentures were not 'personalised'......More..... 'one type will fit all!'

They used to get them ordered from......The good old NHS
It didn't cost them very much......About a pound or less....

These days, it seems the 'must have' is......A perfect dazzling jaw....
With no distinctive features now......Just like in days of yore!

Their gleaming 'beams' are whiter than......New freshly fallen snow....
And if they went out in the dark......I'm sure that they would glow!

The biggest difference I can see......With these new posh veneers
Is now they have to pay much more......To grin between their ears

The cost of these 'improvements' is......Just quite beyond belief!
In fact, I think that you will find......They're paying through their teeth!

I don't like this 'perfection' much......I think it can cause harm
A crooked tooth or gappy smile......Can conjure up such charm!

It seems that 'they' just want to be......The same as all the rest
When really being 'different'......Is often what looks best!

So when you're at the dentist next......Don't go for too much 'style'
Just come back home to those you love......With your own unique smile!
****

During the late Summer, in a morning, I sometimes found silver slug trails on the kitchen doormat and around my cat's nearby food bowl. I can only assume that the slugs were able to squeeze themselves through between the door and frame (which are wooden). One night I went to feed my cat, Daisy.... to find two slugs in her bowl! Neither of us was impressed! However.... inspiration for a little ditty!......

Dinner Date

Two slugs were out a courting
Beyond the kitchen door
One promised to the other....
A meal like none before
"It might be lamb or turkey
Or tuna fish or beef....
But if you want to try it
Then slither underneath....
Beneath the kitchen door there....
But watch out for the cat!...
Her dinner should be down now...
Just over by the mat
The cat is quite obliging
She often leaves a bit
To snack upon much later...
Her Mum will have a fit...
If she comes in and sees you
Sat scoffing on the plate
But isn't this exciting?
A proper dinner date!"

****

One of the things I hate most about people, is the fact that some amongst us have no respect for the environment, dropping litter, and most annoyingly, picking up their dogs' poo, but then slinging the poo bag into a bush or hedgerow. I am a keen litter picker and I wrote this for fellow 'Wombles'……

Super Duper Litter Scooper

All hail my fellow Wombles!
I had a dream last night
About a new invention
To help us with our plight...
A super duper gadget...
An answer to our prayer...
It took the doggy poo bags
And turned them into air!
It was a litter scooper
With magic powers so great
That plastic, cans and bottles
Did just disintegrate!
Now all that I am hoping...
Is that my dream comes true
And if someone invents it...
I'll be first in the queue!
Meanwhile me and my picker
Will keep up with the fight
Just hoping that these litter bugs
Will soon learn wrong from right!

****

2020 seemed to be a good year for yielding fruit. I enjoyed several 'blackberrying' trips around the local hedgerows, and harvested elderberries from my neighbour Ann's garden (with her permission of course)….

Delicious Delights

An early Autumn forage
For blackberries and sloes
Ink stains upon your fingertips
And brambles scratching toes

Bring in your green tomatoes
Your damsons and your plums
So many fruity recipes
To satisfy those tums

Harvest your elderberries
And steep them in some gin
A jewelled delight to sip upon
To let the New Year in!

Get ready for your chutneys,
Your jellies, tarts and wine
Your cakes and pies and crumbles
All tasting so divine

We really should be grateful
For what Nature provides
She gives us the ingredients...
Delicious, true delights!

****

On my poetry writing journey, which began in April 2020, I discovered a style known as 'looping', where the final word on a line becomes the first word of the next line. It is quite fun to do....the next few poems are in this style.....

Smiling

Smiling is what you should do
Do it when you're feeling blue
Blue is bright just like the sky
Sky is where your dreams can fly
Fly to places far away
Away from humdrum everyday
Everyday new things to face
Face is just that special place
Place to wear that smile

****

Autumn Fruits

Autumn fruits are ripening
Ripening berries grow
Grow amongst the hedgerows
Hedgerows full of sloe
Sloe berries and black ones
Ones called elderberries
Elderberries make good jam
Jam is necessary
Necessary for your toast
Toast the brand new season
Season is now Autumn
Autumn is so pleasing!

****

Truth

Truth is what's important
Important must come first
First is where the winners come
Come last is for the worst
Worst thing you can do is lie
Lie is living proof
Proof that you are hiding
Hiding from the truth!

****

Trouble

A trouble shared is a trouble halved
Halved then shared again
Again you share your trouble
Trouble starts to wane
Wane away to disappear
Disappear from view
View will then look better
Better times for you
You will then feel calmer
Calmer brings you peace
Peace will bring contentment
Contentment......trouble free

****

My cat, Daisy, gave me the inspiration for this one…..she has perfected the art of relaxation especially outside on a warm sunny day….

Feline Fine

Cats do like relaxing
Relaxing in the sun
Sun beats down so warmly
Warmly on their tum
Tum is feeling hungry
Hungry means it's time
Time for meat and biscuits
Biscuits for felines
Felines are the pussy cats
Pussy cats feel fine
Fine and dandy happy cats
Cats in the sunshine

****

I adore long tailed tits, they always bring a smile to my face.....usually arriving in my garden in busy little groups chattering away happily to each other. The Derbyshire Wildlife Trust featured this poem on their Facebook page....

Chirpiness

Long tailed tits are happy
Happy little things
Things so full of chirpiness
Chirpiness with wings
Wings enable flying
Flying through the sky
Sky is full of little birds
Birds just flying high
High amongst the treetops
Treetops up above
Above our heads, the long tailed tits
Long tailed tits I love!

****

2020 was a very good year for berries. My neighbour, Ann, has an elderberry bush growing in her garden that hangs over into mine. We decided to have a go at making some 'Elderberry Gin'.... (it was quite a laborious job de-stalking the berries).... It was very nice when done!!....

Elderberry Gin

Pick your elderberries .... De-stalk them patiently
Wash them in some water .... Then have a cup of tea
Go back to your 'jewels' .... Cover them in gin
Put them in a big glass jar.... Watch the fun begin
Add a bit of lemon peel .... Put the lid on tight
Hide it in a cupboard .... Keep it out of sight
Give the jar a little shake .... Every now and then
In a month it will be time .... To fetch it out again
Strain your drunken berries .... Add them to your pies
Heat water and some sugar .... Make a sweet delight
Leave it to cool thoroughly .... Then the final strait
Add it to the flavoured gin .... Then it's best to wait
Leave it for a month or two .... Or even for a year
Then get the tonic standing by .... Here's to Nature.... Cheers!

****

I know that religion can be a sensitive issue, and that there are many differences of opinion relating to what it all means….

Belief

A controversial subject
I know without a doubt….
I don't mean to offend you
But please just hear me out

I am not a 'believer'
I haven't 'seen the light'
But please believe me when I say
I do know wrong from right

All of these different faiths around
I do not understand
Why they all think so differently
About something so grand

I just don't see the reason
Why countries are at war
Why their beliefs and customs
Just leave them wanting more

I do not feel the need to pray
To something I don't know….
But understand for some people
This is the way to go

I love Nature and wildlife
I help folks when I can
I care about the planet
And the future fate of man

I try to live a decent life
I'm honest and polite
I like to live life peacefully....
Don't see the need to fight

I don't have any answers
To why we're on this Earth
Or know what it is all about
And just what life is worth

I can't believe I could be deemed
A lesser human being
Just because I cannot see
What others say they're seeing

We're all 'in this together'
Every woman, every man
To try to make the most of things
To live as best we can

Why can't we all just get along?
Stop questioning the 'whys'
Just live a fulfilled earthly life....
'Cause everybody dies!

Some say there is an 'afterlife'....
A comfort I suppose
But all they have is faith and hope....
The truth is.... no one knows!

I have good friends who practice faith
With fervent dedication
We love each other and respect
Our different observations

I don't mind what your faith is
Or if you choose to pray
As long as you are good at heart
And cherish every day

****

During the Covid19 'lockdowns', people were finding all sorts of things to do around the home, including having a good 'sort out'.....so this is based on what I imagine some people might have found....

Just In Case

I thought I'd have a clear out....
The cupboards in the kitchen
A job a long time overdue
Was this a wise decision?

I'm starting with the bottom one....
The one that's in the corner
Lord only knows what's hiding here....
Might even find Jack Horner!

I'm crawling on my hands and knees....
I can't quite reach the back
I've found some retro Tupperware....
It's all here nicely stacked

I move on to the next one....
It's full of baking stuff....
Not made a cake for twenty years!
It's all festooned in fluff!

Now what about the spice jars?
And all those fancy herbs?
Most of these I just don't use....
They sit here undisturbed

I've never used the bread maker....
Nor the sandwich toaster
Whatever did I buy this for?....
A bloomin' coffee roaster!

I move on to the tinned stuff now....
I find some ancient spam....
A rusty looking tin of soup
And some 'Ye Olde Oak Ham'

What's this?.... a tin of Chappie!
What is the 'best before'?
I haven't even owned a dog....
Since nineteen eighty four!

I'm underneath the sink now....
There are fifteen rubber gloves!
Some dusters and a J Cloth....
Some stuff to kill the bugs

Stuff for worktops, stuff for floors
Stuff to clean the hob....
Stuff for glass and windows
And stuff to clean the knobs!

Why are there all these products?
I just can't fit 'em in!
When my Mum did the cleaning....
She had Ajax, Pledge & Vim!

I'm not sure I've achieved much....
Moved stuff from place to place
I daren't throw it away though....
Best keep it.... just in case!

****

I wrote this for my Mum and Dad, for their 61st wedding anniversary, and in loving memory of Benjy our very special little dog....

 ## The Two Of Us
(Aar If You Like)

He spotted her across the 'rec'....
Where boys and girls would meet....
And so began a lifetime of
A true love so complete

"Can I walk you home?" he asked....
She'd not seen him before....
The answer was "aar if you like"....
Just those four words.... no more

A proper date was then arranged....
To see a cowboy film....
A gentle courtship then ensued....
No need to overwhelm

They'd go for strolls in fields and woods....
She taught him how to dance....
Their friendship blossomed into love....
This was a sweet romance

Two years passed by.... he was called up....
His army days were due
She said that she would wait for him....
It's all that she could do

How could they cope for all that time?
How would it ever pass?
They had no need to worry though....
For their love.... it would last

He was on leave.... they got engaged....
Top deck of a Trent Bus
It was no longer 'you' or 'me'....
But just 'the two of us'

They wrote a letter every day....
To keep their love alive
They knew that if they stayed in touch....
Their feelings.... they would thrive

Two years crept by.... but then he said....
He'd serve for just one more....
Could then save up to 'tie the knot'
With she, whom he adored

This really was a test for her....
She really was distressed....
Could she hold on another year?....
Or would she have regrets?

They persevered for twelve months more....
Then 'de mob' day arrived
Now they could start to make their plans....
To build a future life

A room was spare in Auntie's house....
But this they did refuse....
They wanted to live on their own....
So nothing else would do

They scrimped and saved and saved some more....
Determined to do well
They wanted to find their own home....
A place for them to dwell

Some bungalows were being built....
Could they buy one of these?
They took the plunge and went ahead....
The two of them so pleased

The summer was so long and hot....
Whilst building work progressed
They'd walk around the site at night....
And plan their new love nest

September '59 they wed....
A modest, small event....
No honeymoon, or fancy 'do'....
Their money all was spent

But no two people on this Earth
Were happier than they
They'd saved and waited for so long
For this their Wedding Day

They worked so hard....to make their home....
A happy place to be....
Within two years, 'the two of us'
Turned into 'just us three'

One day whilst he was out at work
A baby girl was born
Their roles in life forever changed
Since he left home that morn

The years flew by in parenthood
With all the joy that brings
Their home was filled with laughs and love
And all their hearts did sing

The little girl did want a dog....
But Mum was not so sure....
Persuaded into having one....
She'd just have to endure

So 'Benjy' came.... a Jack Russell....
Who stole their hearts.... all three
He was a very special dog
He made their home complete

The little girl grew up and left....
To find her way in life
So he and she were left alone....
A husband and a wife

They settled down to once again
Be just 'the two of us'
A gentle, smooth, adjustment....
Without a lot of fuss

Their lives have been so simply led
They've always been content
They really are complete soulmates
To each one.... heaven sent

Throughout the years their love has grown
So strong in every way....
The two of them inseparable....
For ever and a day

****

It seems in general, that the world seems to spend far too much time worrying over image and 'perfection' instead of accepting ourselves and each other for the wonderful individuals that we are…

Self Love

When you look in the mirror....
Is what you really see....
Behind the cloak of flesh and bones
Just who you want to be?

Can you look so intensely....
And peer down deep Inside?
To find just what is hiding there
With both eyes open wide?

Could you be less judgmental....
And more open of mind?
Could you be more compassionate
Considerate or kind?

Accept that you're not perfect....
For what does 'perfect' mean?
Your own view of 'perfection' might....
Not be what others deem

Respect yourself completely....
To your own needs attend....
Be happy being by yourself....
For you are your best friend

Before you can love others....
With all your heart and soul....
Then you must learn to love yourself....
To see yourself as 'whole'

Self love is your foundation....
On which you then can build
Constructing true ability....
To love and feel fulfilled

Self love means self acceptance
You are your unique self
Just love yourself then you can learn
To love somebody else

****

This trilogy was inspired by this photo that I took of my cat Daisy (affectionately known as Daisy May)....we have no cat flap, so when she wants to come in, she sits on the window ledge, and if necessary, taps or scratches on the window.....

Tin Cat

But he is just a tin cat
So how come he's inside?
And I'm stuck here upon the ledge
With quite a cold backside

I think there's something wrong here
It doesn't seem quite fair
I'm sat outside.... it's going to rain
And he's stood smugly there!

I know if I wait long enough
Someone will see I'm cross
Then I'll go in and show that tin
Just who is really boss!

****

Tin Cat - The Reply

I may be 'just a tin cat'....
At least I know my place
And I've been here the longest
So you just 'shut your face!'

Now listen 'ere you fat cat
You just keep getting bigger
And there's one thing for certain
I'll never lose my figure

And 'you' are so demanding
With all that need for fussing
The only thing that I require
Is just a bit of dusting

So yes I am a 'tin cat'
And you're a piece of fluff
And I'm not going anywhere
So you can go 'get stuffed'!

****

Tin Cat - The Truce

Now let's stop all this squabbling!
I've told you both before....
If you can't learn to get along
You'll both be out that door!

There's room enough for both you cats
Inside this heart of mine
You both have different roles to play
To keep me feeling fine

Old Tin Cat you have been with me
Since 1999
You've been a solid trusty friend
And stood the test of time

Now Daisy May you're full of life
And make me laugh each day
I rescued you from Ashbourne Ark
A sad and lonely stray

So you sit there and have a chat
And see where you went wrong
The world will be a nicer place
If you just get along!

****

During the pandemic, I took my Dad to the hospital for a routine check up. The hospital has a very wide, bright and airy central corridor with a glass roof…

Covid Rain

I'm sitting in the hospital
A cup of tea I've had....
The café run by volunteers....
I'm waiting for my Dad

I see him in the waiting room
Across from where I sit
A crazy situation here….
Because of the Covid!

I should be sitting next to him
As he awaits his turn
But rules must be abided now
Hard lessons we must learn

It's just a checkup thankfully
And not something severe
I hope that all will be okay
And nothing to cause fear

I can't help thinking of the folks
Who come here really scared
And have to sit there all alone
As if nobody cared

This virus means that we can't hug
The ones we love the best....
We feel like we're rejecting them....
Go Covid! You're a pest!

Dad's been called in to have his checks....
This special man I love....
I start to think what's happening....
Then hear a sound above

The noise just now is deafening!
The rain is beating down
Whoever chose the roof on here....
They must have been a clown!

It's like I'm at an airport now
Next to a jumbo jet!
And all that's really happening....
The roof is getting wet!

This is a huge design fault here
It really is so loud!
I think I need some earplugs....
All this from one big cloud!

I watch Dad make his way to me
Thank goodness all is well....
So we head for the exit door
But hang on! What the hell?

It's like a monsoon in full flow
Not raining cats and dogs....
It's definitely worse than that!
It's more like cows and hogs!

We're waiting for it to calm down
It isn't very far....
But stupidly.... the umbrellas
Are in the bloomin' car!

We make our way back home to Mum....
This virus is a pain!
I think today it taunted us
And sent the 'Covid Rain'!

****

During the Covid19 pandemic there were times when various restrictions on how we lived our lives, came into force by the way of 'lockdowns' or 'tier' systems. I wrote this in October 2020, prior to the second 'lockdown' and before the vaccines had come into play. People were quick to criticise the government, whatever action they took. It couldn't have been easy deciding how to manage the situation, and whatever choices were made, either the economy suffered, or peoples' lives were potentially put at risk. Some people just refused to take any notice of any instructions or guidance given….

Focus

Let's think of what we CAN do
And not on what's denied
Let's make the best of everything
'Cause some of us have died

Let's stop all of this moaning
And thinking we know best
Let's try to have some common-sense
And bicker a bit less

You think you could do better?
To sort this problem out?
There is no ideal answer here
It's dreadful there's no doubt

The choices are horrendous
Kill people or kill jobs!
There is no perfect balancing
And something must be lost

Whatever is decided
Somebody will lose faith
But Covid's here, we can't deny
It's hard work keeping safe

Let's focus on our home life
And keeping ourselves well
It isn't time for parties now
We're in a living hell!

So let's all pull together
Let's stop messing around
Let's learn to live with this damn thing
Until a vaccine's found!

****

I've often thought that if you're wearing uncomfortable clothing, especially underwear or footwear, then you're in for an unsettled day....

'Undie' Blues

If your 'undies' and your shoes aren't right....
Then a bad day lies ahead
If your bra strap's digging in too deep
Then you'll wish you'd stayed in bed

If your knickers are just getting lost
In a place where the sun don't shine
Then you know no matter what you do
There'll be just no 'feeling fine'

If your bunion's beating like a drum....
And your toes are feeling sore
If the blisters forming on your heels
Mean you can't walk anymore....

Then perhaps it's time to make a change
And dig out your thermal vest....
Find your biggest belly warming pants....
Pull them right up to your chest

When your unleashed boobs are hanging free
And your buttocks feel at ease
Then the world will seem a better place
And you'll feel you've been released

When you're in your comfy underwear
And your favourite tatty shoes
Then you'll feel that you can rule the world
And forget the 'undie blues!'

****

In October 2020, I'd been watching the news, where groups of students had been having huge parties despite the Covid restrictions......above all....rather than feeling angry......I felt totally saddened that we seem, as a society, to have become totally selfish and unwilling to sacrifice anything for the good of the nation as a whole. I keep thinking of some of our ancestors who fought and gave their lives in World War 1 (and indeed subsequent wars). What a waste! ...

Slaves
(Boys In Living Hell)

Young lads in stinking trenches
Gave up their lives and voices
In order for their followers
To have freedom and choices

They went off to the frontline
Determined to succeed
To fight for their whole country
No sense of self or greed

Fast forward ten more decades
They're turning in their graves
Some youngsters in the present
Are nothing more than slaves

Slaves to greed and selfishness
Slaves to drink and drugs
Slaves to self indulgence
Don't care about this 'bug'

They 'need' their student parties
They have no self control
They 'need' their 'life experience'
To make themselves feel whole

It makes me feel so saddened
When I think of those boys
Who lived a life of living hell....
They didn't have a choice

If they were living in this time
They'd choose with all their might
To fight against this virus
To stay at home at night

However did we get to be
So focused on ourselves?
So easily forgotten....
The boys in living hell

****

I joined a Facebook poetry group, where I have been sharing my poems. I have 'met' some really lovely people within the group and although I have no 'Facebook Friends' (in fact I wrote a poem on that very subject, which is in my first book), I have been sharing news and poems with my American 'Messenger Friend', fellow poet... Mark Shifflet. Mark asked if I would like to co-write a poem with him.... I wrote a line then he did and so on....

Only For One Day

I'd like to be invisible but only for one day....
To see and hear what others think about me.... what they say....
But then I might not like what's said, and wish I'd stayed in view
The things that I may hear from them might make me sad and blue

But then again, what fun I'd have just going here and there
Just jumping on a bus or train not paying any fare
I could sit down in comfort there, on someone's empty knee
And laugh as they are freaking out as I drink all their tea

I could eat half their Krispy Kreme, or leave them just the crumbs....
And leave them sitting there so scared and acting kinda dumb
I could then lick their sticky hands, and make them run about
They'll scream out.... "Oh for goodness sake!
What is this all about?"

I'd sneak into smart office blocks.... ripping up their papers
And leave a little 'stinky' so.... they're smelling all my vapours
The 'suited' fancy business types would all turn up their noses
And sit there thinking to themselves...."This doesn't smell like roses"!

I'd go into the shoe store next, and throw them all about....
I'd make them walk across the floor
And watch folks scream and shout....
Invisible might just be fun, but only for one day....
I think it's better to be seen
As I am sure do 'they'!

****

Another combined write with Mark Shifflet....

Distance

We live so far away and yet
Can 'chat' 'most every day
It's hard to think a great big sea
Just gets right in the way

Let's build a bridge above the waves
So we can cross the sea
Then I can see you face to face
And you can then see me

It would take many years of course
To build a bridge so long....
Get everyone to work on it
And sing a happy song

I think the workers would get hoarse
With all those merry tunes
If we've enough to do the job
It might be done quite soon

But this is just a fantasy
And just cannot be done
But just think if it was for real
Then wouldn't it be fun?

So we will have to make the most
Of chatting on 'the net'
Maybe one day we'll get the chance
Of flying on a jet

It's good to chat to those abroad
To learn of different lands
Maybe one day we will meet up
Then we'll be shaking hands

****

Often, some people find it difficult when the clocks 'spring forward' or in this case, 'fall back'....

 Extra Hour

Remember! ....change your clocks tonight!
Or you'll end up confused
Make sure that you 'fall back' and get....
An extra hour to use

Now ....time is precious as we know
What will you do with yours?
You could get up and make a cake
Or scrub the dirty floors

You could lie in for one more hour
Or get up with the lark
You could jog naked 'round the res'
No one will see.... it's dark!

Perhaps you'll put the telly on
And watch what you have missed
Or open that new box of wine
And quietly get.... drunk!

You might just clean the oven out
Or go and bleach the drains
You could go have a bubble bath
To ease those aches and pains

You might just get a bit annoyed....
'What is the point of this?'
Or snuggle down and make the most
Of one hour's sleepy bliss

Tomorrow dawns ....the cooker's wrong....
So is the central heating
And some cars just don't change themselves....
It's really quite displeasing

So later on when bedtime's wrong
And leaves you feeling sour
And mealtimes seem all out of sync
We'll blame 'the extra hour'!

****

35

The introduction to this poem is lengthy, but I think it is a wonderful example, of how, despite the pandemic, with a lot of determination and a little bit of good luck, people can find a different way of making their dreams come true......

At the end of October 2020, I was contacted by an old friend, Sally. I grew up a few doors away from Sally and we often played together as children, and I have also known her husband Scott, since we were all teenagers. I was a bridesmaid at their wedding many years ago. Our adult lives have taken us in different directions, but occasionally, especially more recently, our paths have crossed and we have always kept in touch at birthdays and Christmas. Sally & Scott's daughter, Chloe, was due to be married on 7th November so Sally asked if I'd written any 'wedding' poems (which I hadn't). I said I would 'have a go'. Originally, a big wedding had been planned at a hotel, for around 200 people in total throughout the day and evening, to be followed by a luxury honeymoon in Finland. Of course, due to the Corona Virus, plans had to be changed so, the guest list was reduced to 30, the venue to a registry office, to be followed by a Cream Tea reception. The honeymoon was rearranged to Scotland. I wrote this poem and posted a copy to Sally. However, just as I had posted it, there was an announcement from Boris Johnson about the second 'lockdown' which meant that Chloe & Richard's wedding could not take place! I felt terrible, and wished I'd not sent the poem, but at the eleventh hour, just before Sally actually received the poem, the registry office contacted Chloe to say that they could fit them in the following day on 3rd November. I'm pleased to say that the wedding did take place with just ten guests and they had a lovely day including a nice meal in a hotel restaurant, which the hotel let them have to themselves.....at such short notice! Sally's niece, Catherine, managed to make a cake the day before the wedding and she and another niece, Amy, took it to the hotel without Chloe and Richard knowing, so that was a nice surprise for them. My poem was read out and enjoyed by the guests.

Although I don't really know Chloe and Richard, it was a really nice experience for me to play a small and unusual part in the wedding of the daughter of my old friend.

Covid Wedding Day

The wedding day....not quite as planned....
Because the world's in fear....
A mini version to be held
With those most near and dear

There'll still be vows and wedding rings....
A few well chosen guests....
There'll be a speech and glasses clinked
To wish them "All the best"

No grand reception to take place....
A 'little do' instead....
For two young people so in love
Who just want to be wed

The day will still be one of joy....
With wonders to behold....
More intimate and memorable
For everyone involved

The special honeymoon abroad
Has had to be postponed....
They'll still go off to celebrate....
A bit nearer to home

What really matters in all this....
Is two hearts.... joined as one
Whilst Covid tries to rule the world....
Their new life has begun

Their love will see them through this time
To better days ahead
And they'll recall with happy thoughts
The day that they were wed

****

When I was younger, I used to really enjoy Christmas shopping and giving and receiving gifts, and I know that lots of people still do enjoy the hustle and bustle of it all. I think it used to feel more special because we didn't buy so many things all year round. In recent years (maybe because I'm older), I've found it gets more and more difficult to know what to buy people..... everyone seems to pretty much have what they want already.... or if not, they'll tell you exactly what they want.... you do the same..... so you might as well have just bought your own! I just started to find it a really stressful time and so for the last few years, my family and friends haven't exchanged gifts. Instead, we arrange special get togethers (not necessarily at Christmas), and spend some quality time together doing something that we all enjoy. I know from talking to others that I am not alone in feeling like this. If you do enjoy all the shopping and gift swapping ...then that's great, but it's not for me anymore. It's interesting how your views on things can change throughout your life. I think it's all got a bit too materialistic for me these days.

Christmas Present Blues

Do we need all these Christmas gifts?
Are they a waste of time?....
Much better spending time with folks?
Make sure they're feeling fine?

You traipse around the shops all day
You don't know what to buy
You don't know what the person's got
You feel your brain will fry

You end up spending far too much
Your friends will do the same
Then you exchange the chosen gifts....
Maybe a pointless game?

You end up with unwanted stuff
That you would never choose
And they are feeling just the same....
The 'Christmas Present Blues'

I know it's different for the kids
'Cause Santa Claus is due
Might adult family and friends
Prefer some time from you?

You end up getting 'in the red'
Because of all this farce....
Conditioned into spending lots
By millionaires 'in charge'

Don't spend what you cannot afford....
Agree with those you love....
To spend some time instead of cash....
It will do you all good

Perhaps you cannot meet 'in house'
Whilst Covid's on the scene....
Meet in the park or Facetime them
Or meet through Zoom on screen

Perhaps write Christmas letters to....
The ones who live away
Or phone them up to have a chat
And really make their day

Let's not forget what Christmas means....
To bring goodwill and peace....
To bring to others happiness....
Not just to drink and feast

The best gift you can give this year
Whilst things are so unpleasant
Is share your love and spread good cheer....
Give them your Christmas 'presence'!

****

I think that Halloween celebrations have got a bit out of hand in recent times, and don't think it's right for people to go 'Trick or Treating' randomly knocking on people's doors. It can be quite scary and intimidating for people who live on their own in particular.....but a good subject for a rhyme....

Halloween

Proud pumpkins are a glowin'
Loud poltergeists a throwin'
An ill wind is a blowin'
Because.... It's Halloween!

Black cats are out a prowlin'
Wild werewolves are a howlin'
Damned demons are a scowlin'
Because.... It's Halloween!

Frail skeletons a rattlin'
Old witches are a cacklin'
Small goblins tittle-tattlin'
Because.... It's Halloween!

Pale ghosts are out a hauntin'
The Devil is a tauntin'
The moon.... it's light a flauntin'
Because.... It's Halloween!

The zombies are a creepin'
The broomsticks are a sweepin'
The graveyards aren't a sleepin'
Because.... It's Halloween!

Brave kids are trick or treatin'
They're shoutin' out their greetin'
With buckets to put sweets in!
Because.... It's Halloween!

****

Usually, I go out walking most weekends with a wonderful group of ladies, all ex workmates, six of us in total, who have known each other collectively for many years. We love to celebrate our birthdays (and any other occasion for that matter) with champagne breakfasts, cream teas, theatre trips, or meals out etc. Sadly, during the pandemic, none of that has been possible. It was Halloween and also Sarah's birthday....so we did the best we could, given the circumstances, in one of our local parks,,,,Shipley Park.....

Sarah's Halloween Birthday

Well.... it was Sarah's birthday
And she was feeling low
If Covid wasn't hanging round
We'd know just where to go

Perhaps a champagne breakfast
Or cocktails.... then a show
But seeing as we can't do that
Let's have a think.... I know!

We'll all meet up at Shipley
The 'rule of six' obey
A social distance wander
Then celebrate birthday

The day dawned wet and windy
We waited.... might improve
It did as luck would have it
And so we made a move

We put on boots and wellies....
We squelched across the grass
We got some puzzled glances
From people walking past

Wrapped up in winter woollies....
We took our picnic chairs
We found a spot beside some trees
And sat in open air

....Looked like a witches' coven
All sat there in a round
But we ate cake that we had made
And birthday cheer was found

We also drank some coffee....
We sipped a glass of wine....
Took some photos.... had a laugh
So Sarah now felt fine

We then did go a wander....
To exercise our thighs
The turning leaves were beautiful
And made our spirits rise

We are so very lucky....
This crazy group of friends
We'll make the most of what we can
Until this Covid ends!

****

I wrote this as the second 'lockdown' in November 2020 began….

Can Can

Come on let's do the 'CAN CAN' now
Put 'CAN'T' out of the way
We CAN keep mental health in check
Keep busy every day

We CAN keep talking to our friends
And help each other through
We CAN offer a listening ear
To people feeling blue

We CAN get all those odd jobs done
Clean all those cupboards out
We CAN put on our favourite songs
And have a dance about

We CAN go walking with a friend
Just keeping well apart
We CAN still air our hopes and fears
And have a heart to heart

We CAN try cooking something new
Or bake a favourite cake
We CAN use our creative skills
And see what we can make

We CAN read books and magazines….
Escape from real life
We CAN make plans for future times
When Covid's not so rife

So do the CAN CAN…. raise your skirts….
Lift up your legs sky high
And kick this virus 'up the ass'
Don't let it multiply!

****

43

I don't know where the inspiration for this came from....I'm not a religious person, but I find it hard to believe that the 'essence' of a person, the personality, the individuality, the spirit, soul, or however you think of it, can just disappear when someone dies....

Gone

Just where have 'you' gone to?
Might 'you' still be here?
Are 'you' standing by me....
Whilst I shed a tear?

I know that your body....
Is under the ground
But that's just a vessel
That carried 'you' 'round

Are 'you' now a spirit?....
Or maybe a soul?
Can 'you' still be with me?
Can 'you' keep me whole?

Are 'you' up in heaven....
With others you've loved?
Are 'you' looking at me....
From so far above?

I don't know the answers....
It's all so unknown
I just want 'you' with me....
I feel so alone

What made 'you' a person....
Not just flesh and bones?
Unique individual....
Just one on your own

'You' cannot just vanish
When vessels are worn
Maybe 'you' are waiting
Again to be born

So great are the questions
Is there a big plan?....
Just love one another
Whilst ever you can

For life is so fragile....
One 'blip' and it's done
And then you will wonder
Just where have 'you' gone?

****

I spent many years as a Civil Servant, working in Unemployment Benefit Offices and Jobcentres. The excuses I heard over the years for people being late for appointments were many and varied....

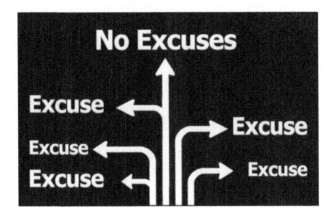

Excuses

For many years I had a job
Where no one wants to go
A place best known in olden times....
'Ye Office Of Ye Dole'

The folks would have appointment times
To sign the dotted line
And if they turned up late at all
I had to ask them .... "Why?"

Excuses.... I have heard them all....
Like dodgy clocks and such....
"The car broke down".... "The bus was late"
"The toilet wouldn't flush!"

"The dog got loose".... "The boiler broke"
"A lorry blocked the street"
"I couldn't find my back door key"
"I had someone to meet"

One bloke, when questioned, said to me
"Been burying my cat!"
(I only hoped that it was dead)
What could I say to that?

Another one, (too much info)....
"I've been having a sh*t!"
I really didn't need to hear
This vulgar kind of wit

I think some were related to
A type of thing feline
'Cause poor old grandad passed away
Some half a dozen times

One bloke announced that he'd been to....
A clinic....STD
He'd wanted to check out that he
Had not caught a VD

Another said that from its cage....
His budgie.... out it got!
He and his wife were so stressed out....
It gave them both the 'trots'

Sometimes 'twas hard to figure out
Just what 'the real truth is'
I could have handed prizes out
For some unique excuses!

If only they had been on time
There would have been no queues
So why did some just turn up late?
There's really no excuse!

****

This is a true story......my partner the car cleaner...... I lived on a main road at the time and had to park on the road......it wasn't always possible to park directly outside my house....

Car Wash

A Christmas trip to Cornwall....
We're all set and we're keen
The day before.... prepare things
And give the car a clean

He goes out with a bucket....
I shower.... and when I'm done
I go look out the window....
Check how he's getting on

He's there with car half soapy
And then I realise....
Oh no! This can't be happening!
I can't believe my eyes!

Yes....it's a blue Fiesta....
But....it's not the right one!
My car is further down the road....
What has he gone and done?

I knock upon the window....
I point out his mistake....
He just picks up his bucket
Oh no! For heaven's sake!

I run downstairs to 'sort it'
"You can't leave it like that!
Whose car is this one anyway?
Be quick!.... They might come back!"

He rinses it with water
Then some old bloke appears
He explains what has happened....
I'm laughing.... I'm in tears

He starts to wash my car now....
The old bloke sets off home....
He waves and toots his 'hooter'....
With just a trace of foam

A good job I did spot this
Or just picture the scene....
My car would still be dirty.... But....
The old bloke's squeaky clean!

****

During the second 'lockdown' in November 2020, I had a walk around the local reservoir one late Autumn afternoon on a truly 'golden day'....

November Day

The sunlight casts a golden glow
On this November day
A frosty nip invades the air
Now Winter's on her way

We may be in a 'lockdown' now
But Nature's unaware
She must wind down her Autumn time
With one last loud fanfare

The brightest leaves about to fall
To leave the trees undressed
Framed, standing proud against the sky
Stark branches do impress

We wait to see what Winter brings....
Perhaps some snow and ice
What Nature has in store for us
We only can surmise

Let's greet our Winter with warm hearts....
Accept what she does bring
Let's find the good in every day
Then soon it will be Spring!

****

When we first had a telephone installed at home in the 1970s, it was very exciting! Prior to this I had to arrange for my boyfriend to phone me at the local phone box at a particular time.....he was also calling from a phone box. These days it couldn't be more different, and now the landline is almost a nuisance, because the majority of the calls received on it are not welcome......

Who's calling please?

When I was so much younger..... And the phone rang in the hall
We all got so excited!..... Couldn't wait to take the call
We'd answer with our number..... Polite and clear in tone
To confirm to the caller that..... Indeed we were at home

The caller could be our best friend..... Or someone else we knew
Perhaps the operator with..... "Long distance call for you"
We might get calls from doctors or..... The dentist or the bank
Or someone phoning for a chat..... Or just to tell us 'thanks'

We'd ring the 'Speaking Clock' for fun..... Or even 'Dial a Disc'
If you were on a 'party line'..... You had to take the risk.....
That neighbours might hear something that..... You'd rather they did not
So for those 'lovey dovey' calls..... The phone box..... off you'd trot

Fast forward half a century..... The phone rings in the hall
'Well who the bl**dy hell is that?'..... Don't want to take the call
"HELLO!" We shout out loudly..... "I can't hear you very well!
No I DON'T want life insurance!..... And you can go to Hell!"

"Have I had any accidents?....YES!..... I've had twenty nine!"
"And I DON'T need a new boiler.....'cause the old one works just fine!"
"My broadband's been hacked into? ..... Well go on then! ..... Cut me off!"
"And NO!.....I don't want PPI!..... So why don't you get lost?"

"I can't tell what you're saying!..... Where are you ringing from?"
"However can you do this job?..... It really can't be fun!"
"What?..... Do I want a funeral plan? Well NO!..... I bloomin' DON'T!
And if you phone me back again..... I'll have you by the throat!"

How ever did we get to this?..... With all these nuisance calls?
We don't seem to have privacy..... Within our own four walls
I wish it was like olden days..... When phones were used to chat
Instead of thinking every time..... 'Just who the Hell is that?'

****

One for slimming club members who couldn't go to their group meetings during the Covid19 'lockdowns', and before anyone takes offence, as a target member of a well known slimming club myself, I do know what it's like.

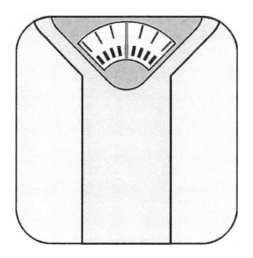

A Good Weigh

You are the one responsible
For what goes in your mouth
So don't start blaming others when
Your belly's heading South!

You've got to find some self control
And keep your lips shut tight
When someone tempts you with a treat
You must resist that bite!

It's no good blaming someone else
For all that cake you ate
'Cause you're the one who pigged it all....
And even licked the plate!

"I don't know why I've gained a pound!"
You say with feigned surprise
When truthfully you know just why....
That chocolate.... and those pies!

You do know what the answer is
To win this weight loss game
Just tell yourself to 'get a grip'
There's no one else to blame!

I know that when all's said and done
It sometimes is quite tough....
But think how really great you'll feel
When you have lost enough!

If you can say you've stayed 'on plan'
For every single day
Aside from something medical....
You WILL have a good weigh!

So come on all you 'fat club' friends
Let's all get back on track
And by the time that Covid's gone
Your trousers will be 'slacks'!

****

I am extremely fortunate to have some very good friends in my life, and I started to think about why we get on so well with some people rather than others...

Friends

What changes strangers into friends?
What makes your minds connect?
What makes you want to share their lives....
To give and gain respect?

Why do you care about them so?
What is it that they bring?
Perhaps a sense of humour.... or
They make you want to sing?

A sense that you are not alone....
Whilst walking on life's path?
A knowledge that whatever's wrong....
They'll try to make you laugh?

True friends will share your ups and downs....
Be there to have some fun
But they'll be there right by your side
When things are looking glum

To know that they are always there
If ever you need help
And in return, you're there for them
To give your time and self

To have good friends.... a priceless gift
To treasure for all time
Please love your friends and cherish them....
I truly value mine

****

I've never been a 'sporty' or competitive person. I absolutely hated and detested any type of Physical Exercise or 'Games' at school. I've always enjoyed walking and dancing, and more recently Yoga and Tai Chi, but that's it....forget the rest!....

P.E. - Not For Me!

I always dreaded "games" at school....
I'd rather have done French....
Detested any kind of sport
It made me feel so tense

I hated every single thing
Connected with 'P.E.'
I didn't want to join a team....
And no one would choose me

When 'Sports Day' came 'round every year
The kids just could not wait....
Except for me.... who loathed the thought....
I'd get in such a state

Now if they'd had a slowness race....
A short jump.... or a low....
Then I could have enjoyed myself
And might have had a go!

If there were prizes given out
For netball 'goal avoid'
Or 'drop the shot put on your toe'
I would have been 'employed'

I tried to run inside a sack
Or in a three legged race
But I would just get all het up
And fall flat on my face

I'd be the one to fall off first
When in the pillow fight
And my boiled egg would leave the spoon
The moment I took flight

Then.... all that running 'round with balls
And vicious looking sticks
In little skirts and navy pants
It just 'got on my wick'

The tennis courts just frightened me
With all those threatening nets
'Cause who would hit them every time?
I'm sure that you can guess

Then they would take us to the 'baths'
To teach us how to swim
But I sat shivering on the side
Not wanting to get in

Now if they'd taken us a walk
Or taught us how to dance
I would have been much happier
And maybe stood a chance

I'm still the same all these years on
I still hate every sport
But I can 'boogie' with the best
And love to go a walk!

****

One for the ladies.......Thankfully, this is not based on a personal experience, but something I read in a magazine, years ago, where readers were recalling embarrassing situations they'd found themselves in.... I've never forgotten it and it could probably happen to any of us...

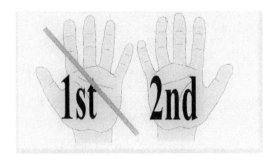

Second Class

She sat there in the waiting room....
Her smear test.... it was due
Anticipating anxiously....
"I think I need the loo!"

She went off to the 'Ladies'.... and
Performed a nervous pee....
She reached out for the paper.... but
The holder was empty!

She felt inside her pockets.... but
No tissues to be found....
She opened up her handbag.... and
She rummaged all around

Receipts galore.... a pair of gloves....
A coupon from a mag....
And a screwed up tatty tissue....
At the bottom of the bag

She made herself presentable
For Doctor's peering eyes....
And she hoped he wouldn't notice
The slight wobble on her thighs

She was called into the room now....
Where she climbed upon the bed
And she tried to 'think of England'
To subdue the feel of dread

She cast her eye around to see....
A desk and frosted window
She gave up all her dignity
With shaking legs akimbo

As she waited for the Doctor
To explore the murky depths
She did sense a hesitation....
Heard a 'clink' upon the desk

The procedure was completed
She put on her shoes and pants....
As she opened up the curtain
She did cast a sideways glance

In a steel dish on the desktop
Right beside a pair of tweezers....
Lay a crumpled sticky postage stamp....
She nearly had a seizure!

The Doctor never said a thing....
She hurried out the door....
Her face was burning crimson
Like it never had before!

Whatever would he think of her?....
The worst thing was.... Alas!
That despite her social standing
That old stamp was second class!

The moral of this story.... girls....
Avoid a similar issue
By always having in your bag....
A brand new pack of tissues!

****

Someone sent me a newspaper clipping of a funny story..... retold here in rhyme......

Shorts & T Shirts

A drive out to the retail park….
A real hot sunny day
A day for shorts and T shirts.... so
Put extra layers away

On entering the parking bay
The car came to a halt
"For goodness sake....what's wrong with it?"
....Must be an engine fault

"You go and do some shopping love....
I'll try to see what's wrong....
I'll catch up with you later on....
It shouldn't take me long"

So off she went with purse in hand
Whilst he lifted the 'hood'...
He hoped that he could sort it out….
She knew of course he would

Much later on she wondered
Just whatever could be wrong
So headed back to find the car
Amidst a giggling throng

His hairy legs were sticking out....
And so was something else!....
She realised his underpants
Were home upon the shelf

She swiftly knelt and tucked his 'bits'
Back tidily in place....
Then she stood up.... and then caught sight
Of hubby's puzzled face

From deep beneath the car emerged
The local car mechanic
His head was bleeding from the knock
He'd had when he did panic!

The moral of this sorry tale
Of things that may escape
Is wear your undies at all times
To keep your 'privates' safe

****

Lets continue with the lighter stuff.......inspired by an old joke I heard retold recently.....

How Old?

Big Nigel was a fitness freak
He liked to keep in trim
He'd go out jogging in the rain
And 'work out' at the gym

Now, Nature had been kind to him....
He had a youthful face
He had a healthy head of hair
No grey.... well just a trace

Some birthday cards arrived for him....
He didn't want a cake
He thought he'd have a healthy treat....
A piece of fillet steak

He told them at the butcher's shop
His birthday was today
They asked him just how old he was....
He didn't want to say

"Well how old do you think I am?"
They told him thirty nine
"Well actually.... I'm fifty two!"
So he left feeling fine

He went off to the bus stop then
Where stood a lady.... old
She said "Today's my birthday....
And I am feeling bold!"

He said "Well it's my birthday too!
But can you guess which one?"
She said.... "If I can feel your 'bits'
Then I can tell.... spot on!"

He really was intrigued by this
And thought she might be mad
But in the name of research....
He let her have 'a grab'

"I think you're fifty two" she said....
"Well how did you know that?"
"I heard you in the butchers shop....
But thank you for our "chat!"

******

I'm sure that in the Autumn of 2020, there was a lot of discussion and indecision about what to do for the best for Christmas. After I wrote this, the rules changed to allow mixing of households on Christmas Day only, instead of the original planned five days. It seems with hindsight, that it just might have been wiser to cancel all 'get togethers' completely after all as we seemed to 'pay the price' afterwards....

Dilemma

Should we really get together....
This year for Christmastide?
I know that Boris says we can....
But take time to decide....

Will five days of celebrations
Undo the good we've done?
Could it cause another lockdown?....
That wouldn't be much fun

Will there be 'irresponsibles'
Who'll get carried away?....
Whilst others will be sensible....
And safe at home they'll stay

Whatever we decide to do
It won't be quite the same....
Not wise to hug and kiss loved ones....
Or play the party games

We really need to think about
What really matters most....
The health of friends and family
Or playing Christmas host?

Maybe it's wise to sacrifice
The things we'd like to do
And look beyond the here and now....
Observe the long term view

If we can show some self control
And tame the festive cheer
Then hopefully we'll ALL have fun
At Christmastime next year

****

I am a keen litter picker, and sadly, sometimes find evidence of drug dealing amongst the rubbish I collect, but then of course, so many of us rely on 'legal' drugs to maintain our good health….

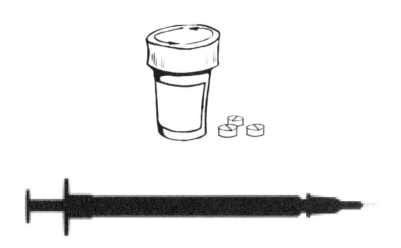

Drugs! Drugs!

Drugs! Drugs! Glorious Drugs!
They are our weapon against evil bugs
They ward off diseases
They take away pain
They combat a virus
They keep people sane

Drugs! Drugs! Torturous drugs!
They are our enemy fuelling the thugs
They start an addiction
They mess up the brain
They cause so much heartache
They drive you insane

Drugs! Drugs! Bewildering drugs!
Used by physicians and also by mugs
In good hands a blessing
In bad hands a curse
An angel or demon
For better or worse

****

Like a lot of people, I wasn't feeling too Christmassy in 2020 with all the restrictions etc, and almost didn't bother to put up my Christmas tree and decorations. However, I gave myself a 'talking to' and did make the effort, and was pleased that I had in the end....

Christmas Rhyme

It's almost Christmastime again
It's time for trees and lights
A time to spread some love and cheer
Despite our current plight

Old Rudolph's nose is extra red....
Has he been on the sherry?
And Santa's looking very round
He's like a giant berry!

Old Frosty's sparkling in the snow
He's proudly standing tall
And people cannot quite believe
The size of his snowballs!

The poor old fairy up the tree
Is looking oh so glum....
But then again how would you feel
With branches up your bum?

Let's raise a glass to all the world
And hope that by next year
Our Christmastime will be 'full on'
Without the Covid fear

****

Unfortunately I have been plagued with 'achy' muscles to some extent for most of my adult life...which with advancing years seems to only get worse.... I try to manage the pain with exercise and massage, but sometimes I just wake up feeling very much the worse for wear. This is my theory......

Alien Abduction

I'm sure that sometimes aliens
Abduct me whilst I snore.....
They take me to their spaceship and
My body they explore

They have a super laser knife
To slice right through my skin....
They turn my muscles inside out....
Then shove them all back in!

They have a magic sewing kit
To hide what they have done
They tuck me back beneath the sheets
When they have had their fun

The reason that I know this fact
Is sometimes when I wake
That every single bit of me
From head to toe does ache

I wish they'd have the courtesy
To put things back just right
'Cause sometimes it just feels as if
I've had a nasty fight!

They seem to be more interested
Since I've been getting older
They really have a preference for
My back and my left shoulder

I wish they'd just leave me alone
And find somebody new.....
Perhaps I'm not the only one....
Maybe they visit you?

****

No one likes a liar…..but how many of us can truly say that we never tell a lie?…..

Liar! Liar!

Liar Liar! Pants on fire!
Or so the saying goes
It's never right to tell a lie
As everybody knows

But can it be ok to lie
If it's for a 'good' reason?
You tell a really massive lie
All through the Christmas season!

You tell the kids….if they are good
Old Santa then will visit….
Of course this is one big fat lie
So that's not right then is it?

You tell them when their teeth fall out
There'll come along…… a fairy
All these 'intruders' in the night
Well…. isn't that just scary?

So if you say you never lie
Perhaps you are a liar
Ashamed now? Are your cheeks alight?
It's just your pants on fire!

******

As I get older, and my feet seem to have 'spread', then comfort often seems to be the most important thing....especially since during the 'lockdowns' I seem to have spent most of the time, barefoot, in socks, slippers, walking boots and wellies!

Ode To Ladies' Footwear

Throughout your life you'll come across so many different kinds....
The ones you'll want to stick with.... and some best left behind

The flashy and enchanting ones you'll love with such a passion....
But attraction often vanishes with ever changing fashion

They'll make you feel so elegant and take you to a party....
But others do the opposite .... by making you feel 'tarty'

Some look plain and boring but support you through each day
And some are really sporty and encourage you to play

They'll have you doing wonders on the pedals of a bike
Or take you through the pleasures of a stimulating hike

Some will leave you walking tall but easily off balanced....
Some serve as decoration.... like a bed might have a valance

Some are nice to look at but are really just for show
And some perhaps are just too high and some are way too low

Some will take you dancing and make you twist and shout
But others you are definitely better off without

Some are old and scruffy but make you feel at ease
And others seem exciting but can bring you to your knees

Some will go the distance.... take you to the highest peaks
And some will cause you so much pain.... leave tears upon your cheeks

Some will make you want to stop and loosen all your laces
The tight ones won't give you an inch and pinch in the wrong places

The cowboy type will make you want to shout a loud 'Yee Haw'
The stiff and rigid army types will just become a bore

Some will leave you feeling so relaxed and warm and cosy
They'll leave you with the feeling that the future's looking rosy

Now when you think of what I've said, and then you think again....
Could it be that footwear is a little bit like men?

****

2020 was undoubtedly a year that none of us could have predicted, and many were keen to say goodbye to. I wrote this on New Year's Eve....

Happy New Year!

A bright, cold, frosty morning
Brings this decade to a close
What 2021 will bring
Is something no one knows

It's safe to say that this year
Has been challenging for most
So tonight, at stroke of midnight
Raise your glasses.... make a toast!

Let's greet the year before us
With a warm and open heart
Let's try to make a happy one
Right from the very start

What's happened can't be altered
And no doubt there's more to come
But remember 'seize the moment'
And when you can.... have fun!

Take joy from simple pleasures
And appreciate what's good
Look around and see the beauty
Don't just 'wallow in the mud'

Try not to be downhearted
For this madness too will pass
Look forward to a better place
With fresh and greener grass

Of course there'll be some sad times
But that's just part of living
Let's focus on the positives....
The loving and the giving

We're all in this together
On this rough and stormy sea
But the coast will soon be clearer....
Look ahead at what could be

Once this current 'spike' is over
And the vaccines stem the flow
Then the future WILL look brighter
With a warm and rosy glow

The days are getting longer
There are signs of Spring to find
So let's welcome this new decade
And leave the old behind

I wish you all good fortune
With a loud resounding cheer
I do wish you most sincerely
A Happy Bright New Year!

****

I wrote this early January 2021, as the third 'lockdown' began…..

LOCKDOWN
Covid-19

Lockdown's Here Again!

So now we have some choices
We could all raise our voices
And make some nasty noises
'Cause lockdown's here again

Or we could all stay calmer
And sit in our pyjamas
And muddle through this drama
Whilst lockdown's here again

Whatever's sent to try us
We cannot let this virus
Defeat and overpower us
Though lockdown's here again

Nobody knows the reason
We're in this 'silly season'
And now it's bloomin' freezin'
And lockdowns here again!

Now let's not get downhearted
Let's finish what's been started
And see this thing departed
Now lockdowns here again!

We'll soon be vaccinated
Then we'll feel less frustrated
And Covid will feel 'tatered'....
We'll start to 'live' again!

****

The kingfisher is usually quite a 'shy' bird, and very fast moving, so sightings and photo opportunities are generally few and far between. After Christmas 2020, along the canal near where I live, one particular kingfisher seemed to quite enjoy the limelight and was very obliging, much to the delight of local photographers. There were many beautiful photos posted on the local Facebook page, and a local artist also painted her first bird.... the kingfisher...

Who's A Pretty Boy?

It seems that there's a film star
Lives Golden Valley way....
Just recently been posing
At some point every day

He's perched and fished quite keenly
And sat on branches proud....
He's really been attracting
A social distanced crowd

I've often glimpsed this fella....
A flash of blue and green....
But with these fancy cameras
His beauty can be seen

Photographers..... I thank you
For capturing this boy
And sharing all your photos
For us to all enjoy

Not only have we photos....
A painted picture too!
Thank you little kingfisher
We really do love you!

Amidst all this uncertainty
And bad news all around
It's once again in Nature
Where magic can be found

****

During one of the Prime Minister's announcements, he mentioned that 'Covid Loves A Crowd'....

Covid Loves A Crowd

We have to stay at home
We chat upon the phone
And have a good old moan
'Cause Covid loves a crowd!

We're missing all our friends
It seems to never end
We can't go out and spend
'Cause Covid loves a crowd!

We must try to be strong
We all must get along....
Don't let it all go wrong
'Cause Covid loves a crowd!

Try not to feel forlorn....
It's darkest before dawn
Look forward to the morn
'Cause Covid loves a crowd!

The NHS can't cope
It's on a slippery slope
So come on ... give them hope!
'Cause Covid loves a crowd!

We WILL get through this mess
Protect our NHS
Vaccines will bring success
'Cause Covid loves a crowd!

****

On 10.01.21 I took my parents for their Covid19 vaccinations.... it made me feel quite emotional.... as I watched a steady stream of cars of mainly 'sixty somethings'... bringing their precious cargoes of elderly parents to hopefully protect them from the evil virus.... also a few more able seniors, bringing themselves, couples hand in hand, steadily making their way to the entrance ......there was a mixed sense of hope, desperation, fragility and most of all love and care......I really hoped that we were turning a corner with the vaccination.

Gold

Today was quite significant
I had a job to do
A most important task required
I had to see it through

I've taken my dear Mum and Dad
To have their Covid jab
I'm feeling quite emotional
Relieved and hopeful.... glad

These two have given all they have
To keep me safe and sound
And now it's time to pay them back
And turn the tables round

I've taken them on their first step
To conquer this disease
Let's hope that this will do the trick
To make us more at ease

I've dropped them off.... I'm waiting now
I watch the scene around
A steady stream of middle aged
Bring loved ones to new ground

The government's been criticised
Throughout this time.... untold
But I for one am grateful....
For them caring for our 'gold'

Let's treasure these.... our precious ones
Who've given us our lives
These vaccinations.... hopefully
Will help us all survive

****

77

It was a miserable, wet, day in January 2021, I nearly didn't bother going out for a walk, but was so glad that I did in the end. It had been so busy around the 'res' and canal because of people exercising locally during the 'lockdown', but there was hardly anyone around on this particular morning...... just beautiful......

Wet Winter Walk

I look out of the window
A wet, cold, misty morning....
Should I go for a wander?
Or stay here warm and yawning?

I really should get moving
So grab my coat and brolly....
My thick socks and my wellies
Should keep me feeling jolly

Canal path now is empty
Too wet for photo shoots
'Sunny' walkers stay at home....
Don't want to wet their boots

The rain falls on my brolly
With a pitter patter sound....
Making bubbles on the water
And puddles on the ground

The raindrops on the branches
Sparkle like fairy lights....
The air smells fresh and 'earthy'
The swan appears.... so white

I'm really pleased I bothered
To set foot out the door....
The beauty on my doorstep
Just cannot be ignored

I head back down 'the valley'
And then.... picture the scene....
The kingfisher lands on a branch
All orange, blue and green

So even when it's gloomy
There's beauty to be found
Just step out into Nature
And take a look around

****

January always feels a long, and at times, miserable month, in the depths of Winter, especially with the added trauma of a pandemic, so I felt that I needed to lighten the mood a little and write a couple of 'silly' poems…. For some reason I woke up one morning thinking of centipedes and shoes….

New Shoes

Imagine if a centipede went shopping for new shoes
Would he buy fifty matching pairs…. or mixed ones would he choose?

He might end up lopsided if he went for different styles
But if he chose some walking boots…. he then could walk for miles

Imagine how much time he'd take to lace them up in bows
I wonder how he'd manage it with no fingers or toes

Perhaps he'd choose a slip on style to save a bit of time
Would he prefer matt leather ones or patent ones that shine?

Where would he put his shoes each night when he lay down his head?
Perhaps he'd line them up beneath his 'centipaedic' bed

As time passed by and it became the time to clean them all
He'd start them in the Summertime and finish in the Fall

Imagine if a centipede could catch Covid19….
He'd put his 'best feet forward'…. and he'd kick it off the scene!

****

Sausage Dog

If 'Sausage Dog' went for a walk in deeply fallen snow
He really wouldn't get too far with little legs so low

He'd envy his Dalmatian friend with legs so long and lean
And wonder on the 'leggy front' why God had been so mean

'Cause what would he end up with whilst he wished that he was tall?...
A chilly chipolata and his very own snowballs!

****

The Covid19 pandemic has undoubtedly been a challenging time for most people, and many will have gone through a very difficult time. I always try to look for the positive in any situation, and I was very lucky to have found my 'poetic voice' during this time which has kept me busy, and allowed me to create and publish not only one, but now two books within less than a year. I wrote this poem when I published my first book 'Lockdown Lyrics' in October 2020......

Book of Rhyme

One day when I am older....
I'll look back on this time
And think of how it led me
To write a book of rhyme

My poet's voice was wakened
By something someone said....
The seed of writing verses
Was planted in my head

I don't know why it grew there
Or if it's here to stay
I just know that it's with me
Throughout each Covid day

It's brought me so much pleasure
And made me some new friends
It's given me a purpose....
I hope it never ends

So somewhere in the future....
Someone may ask sometime
How did YOU cope with Covid?
"I wrote a book of rhyme!"

****

Printed in Great Britain
by Amazon